Frank Muir's What-a-Mess

Frank Muir's
What-a-Mess

Based on Frank Muir's original concept and stories
and Joseph Wright's illustrations

Adapted for television by Tim Forder
Written by Clive Hopwood
Illustrated by Paul Crompton

Contents

From the ITV series produced by Bevanfield Films for Central Independent Television.

Licensed by Link Licensing Ltd.

Copyright © 1990 Central Independent Television plc/What-a-Mess Ltd. All rights reserved.

Published in Great Britain by World International Publishing Limited, An Egmont Company, Egmont House, P.O. Box 111, Great Ducie Street, Manchester M60 3BL.
Printed in Great Britain.
ISBN 0 7235 6878 2

Meet What-a-Mess and Friends

Knock on the door of any palace and you will probably find a prince or two inside. This is not surprising. Palaces are where princes live. Normally, that is. At least one, however, named Prince Amir of Kinjan, lives in a dog basket.

There is a very good reason for this. Indeed, it's the best of all possible reasons. He is a dog, an Afghan hound puppy. He is small, fat and scruffy. And nobody calls him Prince Amir of Kinjan. Everyone, or nearly everyone, calls him What-a-Mess.

Once you've seen him it doesn't take much brains to work out why. His coat is usually uncombed, and full of all sorts of bits and pieces that have somehow become caught up in it. His basket is no better. That is brimming over with all kinds of stuff from old bones to baked bean tins.

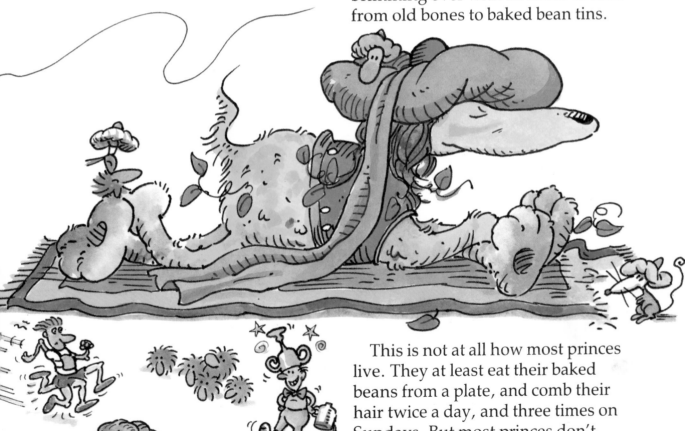

This is not at all how most princes live. They at least eat their baked beans from a plate, and comb their hair twice a day, and three times on Sundays. But most princes don't have half as much fun as What-a-Mess. Nor do they have such interesting friends . . .

5

THE ARCHBISHOP OF CANTERBURY

Equally scruffy, but with no royal connections that he knows of, is the Archbishop of Canterbury. He is a mongrel, and was lucky enough to meet What-a-Mess at the seaside one day.

He is fond of adventures, and is what What-a-Mess's mother would describe as, "Not the right sort of company for a prince!" What-a-Mess, of course, thinks he's just right and he and the Archbishop of Canterbury are the very best of friends.

They both enjoy the same taste in dustbins, chasing cats, and digging for bones. And whenever What-a-Mess is sitting in the misery hole in the middle of the compost heap, the Archbishop of Canterbury can always be relied on to cheer up his best mate with some new, daredevil adventure.

THE CAT-NEXT-DOOR

Although cats and dogs are supposed to be arch enemies, the Cat-Next-Door is actually quite fond of What-a-Mess. But she is a cat, and a cunning Siamese cat at that.

It doesn't help either that the Cat-Next-Door is much cleverer than What-a-Mess. She does rather enjoy teasing What-a-Mess, and manages to land him in all sorts of scrapes. She finds it hard not to like someone who gives her so much to laugh about.

Although What-a-Mess enjoys chasing cats as much as the next dog, he too is fond of the Cat-Next-Door and often plays with her.

POPPET

This sickeningly well-groomed and snooty toy dog is not exactly a friend of What-a-Mess. Indeed, not at all a friend. What-a-Mess doesn't have a good word to say about her. On the contrary, he has rather a lot of bad words to describe her. These are some of them: posh, pampered, sickly, spoiled and scented.

Horrible little squirt. Those are three more. The less What-a-Mess sees of her the better he likes it. He considers Poppet a disgrace to doghood.

CYNTHIA THE HEDGEHOG

Cynthia was rescued by What-a-Mess from being run over by a bus, and they have been bosom buddies ever since. Cynthia, whose name was given to her by What-a-Mess, isn't too sure whether she's a boy or a girl, but likes the name Cynthia very much.

She takes her teddy bear with her everywhere and always has a warm hot water bottle on hand for chilly nights. She calls What-a-Mess 'Watty' for short, and is always willing to help him if he's in any kind of trouble.

RYVITA

Ryvita is a ladybird whose voice is so incredibly tiny even she has trouble hearing herself think. She is, however, very well-read, and is fond of quoting from famous books. What-a-Mess thinks well-read refers to Ryvita's colour, but she doesn't mind a bit and likes him just the way he is.

This is not to mention all of What-a-Mess's imaginary little friends, but you'll only be able to see them if you too can use your imagination like What-a-Mess. Can you see them?

The Archbishop of Canterbury

What-a-Mess and the Daylight Robbery

Princes are born to rule. But as everyone knows, there are always exceptions to every rule. Prince Amir of Kinjan is one such exception.

It wasn't so much that this prince, better known as What-a-Mess, was scruffy. Some princes are exceedingly scruffy. It wasn't that What-a-Mess was fat. At one time you simply *had* to be fat to be a prince at all.

What-a-Mess's problems lay more in what he did. And what he did made him look like he did: a *complete* mess. Other princes (and princesses) had the good sense to open exhibitions, parliaments and buildings so incredibly important and famous that sometimes they were better known than the princes (and princesses) themselves.

What-a-Mess, on the other hand, preferred to open wrapped up leftovers from Sunday dinner. Or tins of rice pudding that someone had forgotten to lick shiny clean. Or bags of quite awful things far too shocking for anyone of a nervous disposition to read about.

Given the choice between opening a school fête and a dustbin there was just no contest. The dustbin won 10-0, with one hand tied behind its back. Which is why, on this particular morning, What-a-Mess was not in the happiest of moods.

"Having a spot of bother?" asked the Archbishop of Canterbury, the little mongrel dog, as he was passing.

BANG! BANG! RATTLE- RATTLE!

9

"Can't get this lid off," complained What-a-Mess, wrestling hopelessly with the dustbin.

Interested, the Archbishop offered to stop and lend a hand. It didn't need What-a-Mess to explain what was so important about getting the lid off. He could smell it from where he stood.

Inside the dustbin lay a feast fit for a king. And a prince and an archbishop, of course. Mountains of tasty morsels, temptingly wrapped in shiny, black plastic to keep all the flavour in. The mouth-watering smells from a week's rubbish wafted across to him on the morning breeze.

Without another word the two dogs set about their joint task with vigour. They pulled. They pushed. They squeezed and eased, and rattled and rolled. No use. The lid stayed firmly wedged.

After a while a thought occurred to the hot and rapidly tiring dogs. By the time the thing was opened they realized they would have no strength left to eat the contents. The Archbishop slumped down by the fence and started to chew idly at a stone.

What-a-Mess refused to give in. The Archbishop pointed out that the lid was well and truly jammed. What-a-Mess struggled on. The Archbishop observed that the dustbin three doors down had no lid and was usually good for a couple of half-eaten chops on a Tuesday. What-a-Mess was deaf to his promises.

The Archbishop said that if the dustbin was left for a day its insides would taste even better. He added that if they waited someone would certainly take the lid off for them and might not put it back on so firmly.

"That's just what I fear most," said What-a-Mess, mysteriously. He gave the dustbin a final kick and sat down beside his friend. It was time to reveal what he knew.

What-a-Mess had uncovered a daring and dastardly plot. Every day the man or woman of the house would carefully wrap up all the lovely rubbish. Then they would place it in the dustbin, inside another bag, and seal it with the lid. It was probably the safest place they could think of keeping it.

What-a-Mess knew how precious the man and woman thought it was. They were always saying to him, "Leave it alone!" or "Get out of the bin at once!" whenever What-a-Mess tried to make off with any rubbish.

The trouble was it was being stolen from under their very noses. And in broad daylight!

"That still doesn't tell me why it needs to be opened today," said the Archbishop of Canterbury, lazily tossing away the stone. He turned to chew his back leg for a while, by way of a change.

"That's the whole point," said What-a-Mess, excitedly. "Today's the day!" It had taken careful working out, but through observation and deduction, What-a-Mess had cracked the mystery of the disappearing rubbish.

"Every week, on the same day, they come with a big lorry," he explained. "They sneak up the road while everyone is out at school, or work, or the shops, or doing the washing, or –"

"And then what?" asked the Archbishop, in between mouthfuls of wet leg.

It was too late to explain further. A large lorry turned into the street. Men jumped from the cab wearing overalls and gloves. Some of them even had masks on. Swiftly they ran into the gardens, broke open the dustbins, and ran away with black bags of rubbish over their shoulders.

They stacked them up in big piles by the roadside. Next minute along came the lorry, and within seconds the bags were gone. A brilliant scheme. It had cunning. It had surprise. And it had to stop.

"Plan B," whispered What-a-Mess through clenched teeth.

The Archbishop, ears alert, let the soggy foot drop from his open jaws. He could hardly believe what he saw. There were enough bags of rubbish to feed an army, and still have enough left over for a snack before bedtime.

What-a-Mess eyed the growing hoard of bags in the road. The Archbishop looked too. They exchanged glances, and nodded. "Plan B."

The dustmen had almost finished emptying all the bins in the street. A small pyramid of shiny, black bags, filled to bursting, stood ready for collection by the lorry. The men chatted quietly amongst themselves. Not a soul stirred in the street.

12

With the sound of a thousand gerbils (who have just been told that the first one to break the World Noise Record will get a free carrot) What-a-Mess and the Archbishop of Canterbury burst upon the still, morning scene.

The two forces faced one another across the bags of rubbish. What-a-Mess bared his fangs and growled. The Archbishop did an impression of a Halloween mask that had frightened him as a puppy. It worked.

The men began to talk loudly to each other. One of them advanced with his hand held out. The Archbishop in turn showed him the soggy leg, with an unspoken warning that this could happen to him if he didn't play his cards right and back off.

What-a-Mess decided on more energetic action. Lunging wildly into the middle of the stack of bags he began ripping open every one he could get his teeth into.

The mouth-watering aroma of a thousand discarded dinners soared through his senses. But on he went regardless. There would be time to eat later. What was important was to stop the robbery.

Ten minutes later it was all over. All over the street. What-a-Mess had reduced the pile to nothing. Not a bag lay unopened, not an inch of ground untouched. The contents of fifty eight dustbins lay thoroughly scattered across the entire road from the door of No. 10 as far down as the post-box.

The breeze caught an empty crisp packet and tossed it in the air. Wearing a temporary crown of old orange peel and cabbage leaves, What-a-Mess peered out from beneath some wet cardboard and a bag of something very, very squishy. The street looked like a tornado had hit it. The men had gone.

What-a-Mess smiled contentedly. This would be a day to remember. 'Dog Hero Foils Robbers' the headlines would say "The man of the house will thank me this time," said What-a-Mess with the confident air of someone who has just swum the Channel backwards and one-handed.

"Well," said the Archbishop, looking at the tip and suddenly remembering something terribly important he had to do somewhere else. As a souvenir of the adventure he took a parting snack from one of the handily opened bags.

What-a-Mess couldn't understand why his friend had beaten such a hasty retreat. He was even more puzzled some hours later, as he sat extremely miserable in the misery hole, underneath the compost heap. "I don't understand the world," he said to no one in particular. "I stop a daylight robbery. I save all their precious rubbish. Then everyone shouts at me and they throw me out in the garden without any tea!"

What-a-Mess sighed. Which is, oddly enough, what most princes tend to do at the end of a long and busy day.

14

The Bone Game

A game for 2-4 players. You will need six small counters and one large counter each, and a dice.

Choose your starting place and throw the dice to decide who goes first. Use your large counter to move with. The aim of the game is to collect as many bones as you can by landing on the circles which have bones on. Every time you land on a bone leave one of your small counters on the circle. No one else can claim this bone even if they land on it as well. The first player to collect six bones wins.

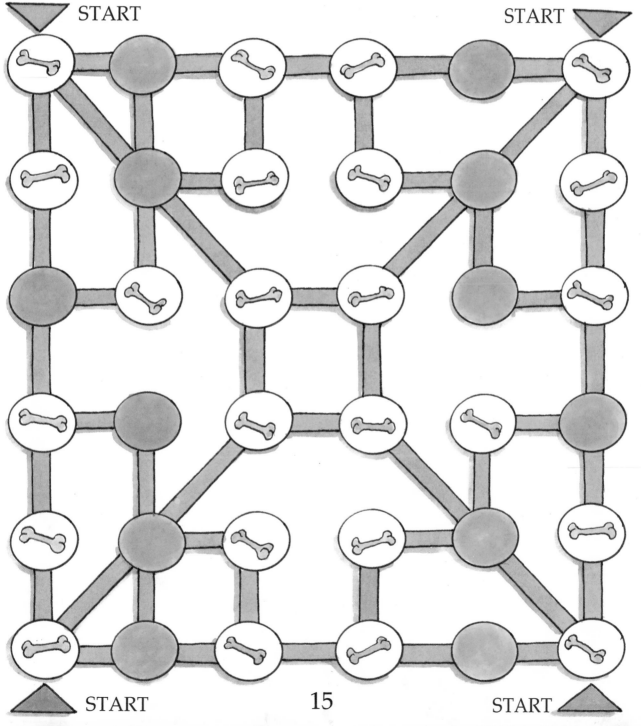

START

START

START

START

What-a-Laugh

What happened to the man who took his dog for a walk along the gutter?
He fell off the roof.

What happened at the flea circus?
A dog came on and stole the show.

What always follows a dog?
Its tail.

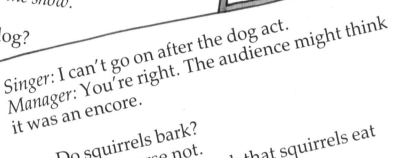

Singer: I can't go on after the dog act.
Manager: You're right. The audience might think it was an encore.

Boy: Do squirrels bark?
Girl: No, of course not.
Boy: But it says in this book that squirrels eat acorns and bark.

What do you get when you cross a dog with an elephant?
A very nervous postman.

Did you hear about the dog who limped into a saloon in the wild west?
He said out loud, "I'm looking for the critter who shot my paw!"

What did the cowboy say when his dog left him?
Doggone!

What do you get when you cross a jelly with a sheep-dog?
Collie-wobbles.

What happens if you cross a dog with a hen?
You get pooched eggs.

It's a Dogs Life

That noble Afghan puppy
Prince Amir of Kinjan

Known to all as What-a-Mess
Enjoys life while he can.

His basket may be scruffy
And filled to great excess,

Though very humble it may be
It's home to What-a-Mess.

There's such a lot to learn about
The world and all its ways

It keeps a dog like What-a-Mess
Quite busy through the day.

Friends to play with all day long:
A hedgehog, dog and cat,

A ladybird, and smaller chums
All doing this and that.

The garden has its uses:
To run and play, explore;

A misery hole to sit and sulk
Is what the compost's for

Bones to bury, bones to find,
Things of wonder too,

Gates and hedges, fences,
To stick your noses through.

Postmen, dustmen, paperboys
Make up a busy day:

Such a lot of visitors
That must be chased away.

And any fearless guard dog
Must have a fearful bark.

What-a-Mess likes practising
By howling in the dark.

So if the world's in chaos
There springs to mind one name...

Yes, you can bet that What-a-Mess
Will surely be to blame.

It's tiring, is a dog's life
There's such a lot to do.

But I think I'd like to be
Like What-a-Mess – don't you?

21

The Cat-Next-Door

What-a-Mess and the Rainy Day

Outside the sky was full of dark, grey clouds. That fat and scruffy puppy, Prince Amir of Kinjan, better known to the world as What-a-Mess, gazed longingly at the garden through the window.

"But why can't I go out, Mother?" he asked for the hundredth time that morning.

His mother told him, also for the hundredth time that morning, that it was raining. What-a-Mess sighed. He *knew* it was raining. He could see for himself. What he wanted to know was *why* he couldn't go out. What was it about rain that meant that he had to stay shut up indoors? He was eager to learn for himself: he wanted to go outside to find out.

What-a-Mess settled down unhappily in his basket, rearranging a half-chewed sock, two bones and a squeaky dolphin that had somehow wedged themselves underneath him. It had been raining for hours and What-a-Mess was bored. He wanted to go out and play.

What was worse was that he had spotted his mongrel friend, the Archbishop of Canterbury, having a great time chasing the Cat-Next-Door round the garden. They could go out when it was raining, so why couldn't he?

"Mother," began What-a-Mess, trying to look his most adorable and rubbing his head affectionately against his mother.

"Later," said his mother, demonstrating her skills as a mind-reader. "Now do stop bothering me."

What-a-Mess sighed even more deeply, resting his chin on a piece of beefburger he'd found a few days earlier and was saving up in case he got hungry during the night. If only someone would let him go outside he'd gladly stop bothering anybody.

Life wasn't easy being a puppy. Everyone was always telling him not to lie here, not to stand there, not to chew this, not to scratch that, not to make a noise, not to talk with his mouth full… in fact, almost everything What-a-Mess did seemed to be not allowed. He sometimes wondered why humans bothered to keep dogs if they were so much of a nuisance.

Just then the man of the house opened the back door and went out. As luck would have it he left the door tantilizingly ajar. What-a-Mess looked round to see if anyone was watching. There was no one else about. With one bound he was free. It actually took him a little while to disentangle himself from his rubbish-strewn basket and at least four bounds, a slide and a lollop to get to the door. But he was most definitely free!

Something was wrong. From inside the house he had quite plainly seen lots of drop-like things falling out of the sky. He had watched them bouncing off the path, pinging off the dustbin, and running down the garage roof. Now he was outside there was no sign of them anywhere.

He resisted the temptation to go back inside and check that he hadn't been imagining it all. He didn't want to risk being shut indoors again. Maybe it was raining somewhere else in the garden. That must be it, he decided. He set off down the path to see if it was raining down there.

Just inside the greenhouse he spotted Ryvita, the ladybird, who was sitting on a tomato plant. She was quite the easiest person to spot that What-a-Mess knew, since she had black spots all over her red wings.

"Hello," said What-a-Mess, greeting his little friend cheerily. Ryvita said "hello" back, but because her voice was so tiny nobody could hear her.

What-a-Mess explained that he had come outside to find out about rain.

"   ," said Ryvita, wisely, or to put it more loudly, "Into every life a little rain must fall." What-a-Mess couldn't hear her, of course, but he did hope it would rain again. It had all been very disappointing so far. Anxious to get on, he bid Ryvita farewell and went on his way.

Next to the greenhouse lay an upturned wheelbarrow. Beneath it, one eyelid slightly open, the Cat-Next-Door peered out from the darkness.

What-a-Mess stopped and looked up at the sky, and then down at the wheelbarrow. "Is it raining in there?" he asked.

"Of course not," said the Cat-Next-Door. "I'm sheltering, that's what I'm doing."

"Are you sure it's not raining in there?" insisted What-a-Mess, who thought the Cat-Next-Door might be trying to fool him. "Can I see?" Without waiting for an answer he wedged his nose into the gap between the wheelbarrow and the ground and tried to wriggle his way inside.

Of course he was far too big to squeeze through such a small space. All that happened was that he overbalanced the wheelbarrow, which toppled gently sideways through the side of the greenhouse, breaking several panes of glass.

The Cat-Next-Door tut-tutted. "Thank you very much," she said. "Where am I going to shelter now?"

25

"Shelter from what?" asked What-a-Mess, staring intently at the inside of the wheelbarrow. There were no drop-like things in there. It was as dry as a bone, or at least as dry as a bone that hasn't been recently chewed.

"The rain, of course," said the Cat-Next-Door, in the tone of voice one uses when answering someone who's just asked you why you don't wear a wellington boot on your head.

"But it isn't raining," said What-a-Mess, "is it?" He wasn't really too sure about this rain business, and didn't want to appear completely stupid.

"It was," said the Cat-Next-Door. "Besides I can shelter from it *not* raining if I like. It is a free world."

What-a-Mess nodded and made a face as if to say he understood perfectly, which, of course, he didn't. The Cat-Next-Door wasn't that easily fooled.

"Come with me," she said, mischievously. "I know exactly where to find some rain." She set off at a brisk trot down the garden.

"Oh good," said What-a-Mess. At last he was going to find out. What it was to have good friends who didn't mind letting you in on a few secrets. He scampered off after the Cat-Next-Door, eager to learn more.

They came to a halt by two trees from which was slung a hammock that had been left out. The Cat-Next-Door raced up one of

the tree trunks and positioned herself comfortably in a hollow between the branches.

"Is it up there?" asked What-a-Mess, not too sure he liked this. His memories of climbing trees were not happy ones. At least, climbing up was all right. It was the getting down bit he had trouble with. He didn't seem to have enough legs to manage it.

26

"No," said the Cat-Next-Door. "You stay there. I'll show you. Now, first things first. Rain falls from the sky."

"Why?" asked What-a-Mess. "What's it doing up there in the first place?"

"Rain has to be kept somewhere," said the Cat-Next-Door. "If it was all down here we should have to swim about all the time. Now pay attention."

"I see," said What-a-Mess. A sudden thought occurred to him. "Why does rain fall downwards? Why can't it just stay where it is?"

"Because the clouds would be far too heavy," explained the Cat-Next-Door patiently. "They'd

all sink to the ground and then we'd all be walking round in fog all day, obviously. If it all stayed up there the ground would be as dry as a bone, and no plants would grow."

What-a-Mess knew about bones. He was about to mention bones that had been recently chewed, but thought better of it. He tried to look as if it all made sense to him. "So," he said slowly, "rain is wet."

"Brilliant," said the Cat-Next-Door, and smiled the way cats smile when they know something you don't. "Do you want to see?"

"Oh yes please," he said, full of enthusiasm. The Cat-Next-Door grinned and helpfully positioned What-a-Mess for the best view. "Left a bit, right a bit, stop." It took a little time while What-a-Mess worked out which was his right and which his left, but eventually he was ready.

"Is it going to rain now?" asked What-a-Mess, looking upwards with an air of anticipation. "I don't see any yet."

"Here's some I prepared earlier," said the Cat-Next-Door. "Are you ready?"

What-a-Mess nodded and waited expectantly. The Cat-Next-Door lazily stretched out a paw and gently rocked the hammock. After all the recent rain it was full to the brim. Little drops began to spill from the sides.

"That's it!" cried What-a-Mess in excitement. "That's just like what I saw through the window."

27

"Would you like some more?" asked the Cat-Next-Door, who was beginning to look like a big smile with a cat on the end of it. "Here it comes." With one or two more energetic swings the whole hammock tipped upside down and emptied itself all over What-a-Mess.

"W-w-wow!" said What-a-Mess, soaked from head to foot. "It *is* wet."

"Quite correct," said the Cat-Next-Door. "Rain usually is. Just let me know if you need any more lessons. Goodbye. Time for my afternoon zizz." She bounded off, laughing like a drain. (Drains don't laugh too often, but when they do, they do it just like the Cat-Next-Door.)

What-a-Mess thanked his cheerful friend and made his way back to the house. He knew his mother would be very keen to hear what he'd learned about rain. He slipped through the back door and found his mother in the living room, lying curled up in front of the fire.

"Look," he said, shaking his coat enthusiastically. "Rain is wet."

And seconds later, so was the living room. Exceedingly wet. And curiously, nobody seemed in the least bit interested in what he'd learned about rain. Maybe there was more to it than he thought. As Ryvita said later, "   ," which, roughly translated, meant, "A little learning is a dangerous thing."

What-a-Laugh

Where do Eskimos keep their dogs at night?
  In a mushroom.

Man: My dog thinks he's a chicken.
Friend: Shouldn't you take him to a vet?
Man: I would, but we need the eggs.

What do you get when you cross a long-haired, overweight, soaking wet dog with a cat wearing outsize trousers?
  A shaggy, saggy, soggy, doggy, baggy moggy.

Two cats met in an alley. "Miaow," said one. "Bow wow," replied the other. "What are you on about?" asked the first. "That's dog talk."
"I know," answered the other. "I've taken up foreign languages at school."

There was a man called Rover Legplant who once thought he was the Hound of the Baskervilles. A friend asked him how the treatment was going. "The doctor's cured me," said Rover. "I've stopped chasing cars and biting people. I don't search dustbins or sniff at lamp posts any more. I'm absolutely fine now. Just feel how cool my nose is."

Teacher: This composition, 'My Dog', is exactly the same as your brother's.
Pupil: I know. It's the same dog.

How does a dog with a sore throat feel?
  Ruff and yelpless.

What do you get if you cross a pet dog with a jeep?
  A Land Rover.

29

Good Enough to Eat

While What-a-Mess loves a delicious rampage through the dustbin, even more he enjoys an occasional tasty titbit from the woman of the house. You can learn how to make three of What-a-Mess's favourites by following these easy recipes, with a little help from your mum or dad.

DOG BISCUITS

At least that's what What-a-Mess calls them, because he thinks they're all for him!

What you need: 100g (4oz) butter
100g (4oz) caster sugar
1 egg
200g (8oz) plain flour

1 Preheat the oven to Gas Mark 4 or 350°F/180°C.
2 Mix together the butter and sugar with a wooden spoon in a large bowl.
3 Beat the egg in a small bowl and add it to the butter/sugar mixture.
4 Sift in the flour and fold into the mixture lightly.
5 Lightly flour a pastry board and roll out the mixture with a rolling pin to about 3mm (⅛ inch) thick.
6 Cut out some bone shapes from the rolled out mixture.
7 Bake for about 15 minutes until crisp and golden. Leave to cool on a baking tray and sprinkle with a little extra caster sugar.

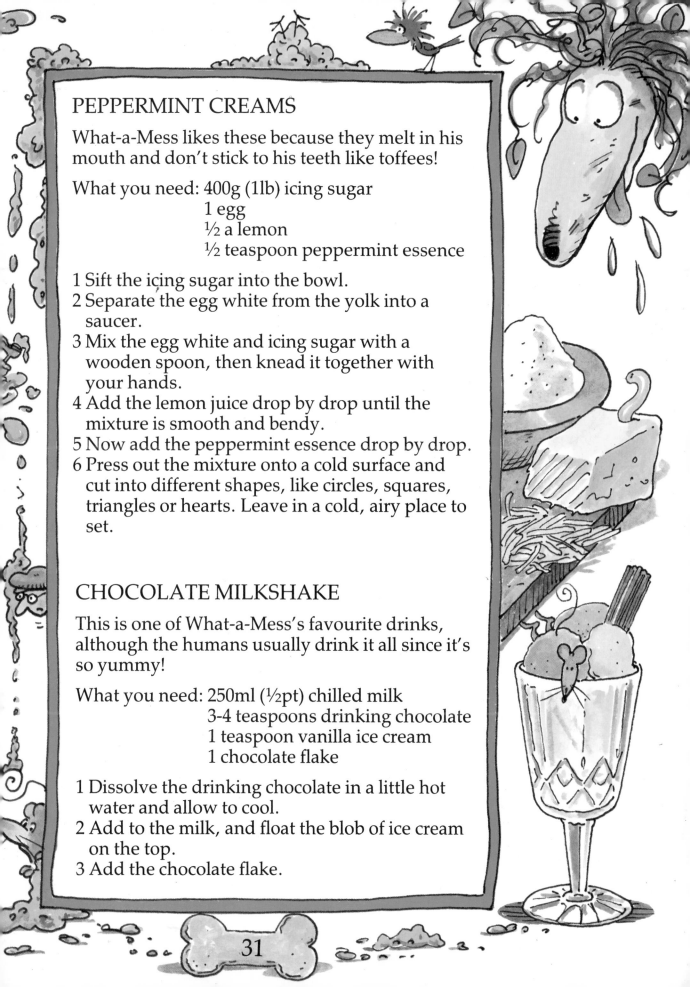

PEPPERMINT CREAMS

What-a-Mess likes these because they melt in his mouth and don't stick to his teeth like toffees!

What you need: 400g (1lb) icing sugar
1 egg
½ a lemon
½ teaspoon peppermint essence

1 Sift the icing sugar into the bowl.
2 Separate the egg white from the yolk into a saucer.
3 Mix the egg white and icing sugar with a wooden spoon, then knead it together with your hands.
4 Add the lemon juice drop by drop until the mixture is smooth and bendy.
5 Now add the peppermint essence drop by drop.
6 Press out the mixture onto a cold surface and cut into different shapes, like circles, squares, triangles or hearts. Leave in a cold, airy place to set.

CHOCOLATE MILKSHAKE

This is one of What-a-Mess's favourite drinks, although the humans usually drink it all since it's so yummy!

What you need: 250ml (½pt) chilled milk
3-4 teaspoons drinking chocolate
1 teaspoon vanilla ice cream
1 chocolate flake

1 Dissolve the drinking chocolate in a little hot water and allow to cool.
2 Add to the milk, and float the blob of ice cream on the top.
3 Add the chocolate flake.

Spot the Difference

What-a-Mess and the Archbishop of Canterbury are very busy looking for a bone that What-a-Mess remembers burying . . . somewhere. There are 10 differences between the two pictures. Can you spot them?

Answers on page 60.

What-a-Mess and The New Basket

Princes are not usually small, fat and scruffy. But some of them undoubtedly are. Such a one is Prince Amir of Kinjan, otherwise known as What-a-Mess.

What bliss! My warm old basket at home and a seat in the country!

What more could a dog ask for?

Suddenly there was the sound of human voices...

It simply has to go. It's falling to pieces and besides it's much too small.

I'll throw the old one away.

I'll buy a new basket

A new basket?!

Throw it away?!!

What-a-Mess doesn't wait to hear another word.

Too-bee, too-bee

Hello Kenneth Coo-jee-coo

What-a-Mess

WHUMP!

What-a-Mess runs into his friends quite unexpectedly.

Yes.

So they are going to throw away my old one and make me sleep in a wire basket under a pram.

When they'd all recovered What-a-Mess told them the whole story.

It was total defeat.

OUTSIDE! NOW!

What-a-Mess retreats to the misery hole.

What am I going to do?

What does it feel like to be an idiot?

The man was throwing out an old **laundry** basket. And it was the baby's new pram they were discussing. **Your old basket** is safe

If you bothered to stop and listen for a moment you wouldn't get into such a mess.

The cat-next-door explained.

What-a-relief!

For this relief much thanks

What-a-Laugh

Teacher: Can a dalmation change its spots?
Pupils: No, Miss.
Girl: My dalmation can. Every time he gets tired of one spot he just stands up and moves to another.

Boy: My dad's so rich he bought a dog for me.
Girl: So what? My dad's so rich he bought a boy for my dog.

Girl: How much are those doggies in the window?
Salesman: Thirty pounds apiece.
Girl: How much for a whole one?

Girl: Look at the dog I got for my brother. I'm going to go back to the shop tomorrow and see what they'll give me in exchange for my sister.

What do you get when you cross a lion with a cuddly Dandemont terrier?
A Dandylion, but if it says "Woof!" stay exactly where you are and listen.

What do you get when you cross a dog with a man-eating spider?
An animal that eats people, buries their bones and lives under your bed.

Which small dog is extremely dangerous?
A chihuahua in charge of a machine gun.

A dog walks into a restaurant and sits down to read the menu.
A waiter comes up and says, "This is amazing. I've never seen a dog sitting at a table in this place before."
"I'm not surprised with these prices," replies the dog.

Dog's Delight

A dog is one of the most loving and rewarding of pets. If you love and care for your dog it will be a lifelong friend.

Owning a dog is a big responsibility, however. A dog needs feeding, exercising and grooming if it is to stay healthy and happy – just like you. This is an important job, and your dog relies on your help to look after it. However much you want a dog, never buy one unless you are sure you can care for it: to do otherwise is very cruel.

WHAT SORT OF DOG TO CHOOSE

When you buy a puppy you should always remember that it will very soon grow up to be a dog. If you live in a small house or flat it would be unwise to buy a puppy that will become a big dog, because there won't be enough room for it.

If you can afford to buy a pedigree dog, like What-a-Mess (pedigree dogs are more expensive), it will be easier to tell what it will grow up to look like. If you buy a mongrel, like the Archbishop of Canterbury (a mixture of different kinds of dogs), it is harder to tell unless you know what its mother and father look like.

A little dog like a chihuahua can weigh as little as four pounds. A very big dog like a St. Bernard can weigh as much as 170 pounds! Some dogs can be very lively and playful, others are quieter and easy going. There are all kinds of dogs, so it is wise to think carefully about which sort would suit you and your circumstances best.

A long-haired dog, for example, will need to have a lot more attention paid to its coat than a short-haired one. You should also think about whether you want a male or a female dog, since a female may have puppies.

So, think carefully before you buy. Do you have time to look after your dog? What sort of dog best suits where and how you live? A dog will be with you for the whole of its life, and you want it to be happy, so take your time and choose wisely.

FEEDING YOUR DOG

Like What-a-Mess, dogs will eat almost anything if you let them, but regular, well-balanced meals will help to keep your dog fit and healthy.

The cheapest and most sensible way to feed your dog is to buy the canned or packaged food that is sold at the petshop or local store. The ingredients in this have been carefully worked out to ensure that the dog receives everything it needs.

Dog biscuits and cereal mix should also form part of the diet, and you should always make sure there is a bowl of fresh water to drink from. Between them these provide all a healthy dog needs.

Take into account whether your dog is large or small, grown up or a puppy, since different dogs require different daily amounts of food, just like different humans do. Read the instructions on the tin or packet, or better still ask your vet for advice.

A few titbits are always a treat for a dog, but be very careful not to ruin its appetite or unbalance its diet.

Don't spoil it like Poppet! Some things that you like may make your dog poorly, and things like toffees can be very dangerous for a dog.

All dogs like bones, because they enjoy chewing them and sucking out the marrowbone jelly. Some bones like chicken bones, however, will splinter and may harm your dog, so select them carefully.

CARING FOR YOUR DOG

Not all dogs need baskets but they help discourage your dog from using the furniture, and give your dog a place that it can think of as its own. A warm blanket it can cuddle up in will help, and be sure that its sleeping place is away from draughts.

Brushing your dog regularly, especially if it is a long-haired variety, will help to keep its coat clean and glossy. Bathing your dog can be quite an adventure, but so long as you make sure it is thoroughly dry before you let it out in the open air it will do no harm. And it will ensure your dog doesn't become too dirty or smelly.

A dog needs to go to the vet's sometimes just like you need to go to the doctor's, especially when it is a puppy. The vet will give it all the injections it needs to protect it against the different dog diseases. The vet will also be happy to advise you and answer any questions you may have about looking after your pet.

Regular exercise is very important, and the bigger the dog the more exercise it needs. The best place is a park or an open space where it can run about, but always keep it on a lead if you are in any doubt.

You must make sure you train your dog to obey your commands without hesitation. Take your puppy to a dog training school when it is young. You will find your dog will enjoy learning so long as you are firm and reward it when it does well.

A well-cared for, obedient dog will be a happy, affectionate and loveable companion for many, many years.

41

Cynthia

What-a-Mess Lends a Helping Hand

"What-a-Mess!" boomed a loud, not very friendly voice.

The noise bounced off the garage roof, rattled the glass in the greenhouse, rebounded from the garden fence, and was on its way back into the house when it passed What-a-Mess, on his way out through the kitchen door.

The woman of the house was not pleased. She was so not pleased that it never occurred to her that this was not the way to speak to a prince. It would be hard to imagine anyone less like a prince, but What-a-Mess was indeed Prince Amir of Kinjan.

And he'd just been turfed out of the house. It had all been a ghastly mistake, of course. What-a-Mess had only been trying to help, really he had. Only the night before his mother had been talking to him about helping others.

She had pointed out to What-a-Mess that his basket was now full to overflowing. Every day the woman of the house had to tidy up all the bits and bobs that were forever falling out of the basket and littering the floor.

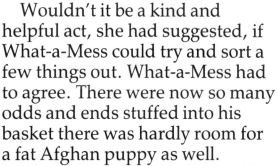

Wouldn't it be a kind and helpful act, she had suggested, if What-a-Mess could try and sort a few things out. What-a-Mess had to agree. There were now so many odds and ends stuffed into his basket there was hardly room for a fat Afghan puppy as well.

When he went to bed it was like climbing the north face of Mount Everest, and What-a-Mess had never had a head for heights. He decided he would have to get rid of a few things.

43

This was easier said than done. It had taken a lot of hard work to collect all these valuable possessions. Trying to decide which to get rid of and which to keep was almost impossible. What-a-Mess couldn't go to sleep for thinking about it.

Then he had a brainwave. What-a-Mess's brainwaves wouldn't win prizes at the best of times, but the ones he has in the middle of the night are the worst of all. And this one was even worse than most.

What a kind and helpful thing, he thought to himself, if I do it all while everyone's asleep. When they woke up in the morning they would be amazed and delighted at how much tidier his basket was.

First, he emptied the basket on the floor and laid everything out. He decided he would have to be strict with himself and allow only twenty things back into the basket. The trouble was he lost count after seventeen, and started from one again.

By the time he had finally managed to count to twenty there were only two things left outside the basket. One was his blanket, and the other was What-a-Mess himself. The pile of things in the basket looked higher than ever.

He started again. It took ages and ages and at the end of it What-a-Mess fell fast asleep. Instead of waking up to the sound of thanks, What-a-Mess was surprised to hear his name being shouted from upstairs. The voice didn't sound too friendly.

Funny he thought. The bath had seemed the perfect place to store all his spare things. It had been empty after all. Clearly no one else was using it to keep things in.

He opened his eyes blearily. The room looked like a rag-and-bone yard that had been hit by a hurricane. Several times. Then What-a-Mess remembered. He had been so tired after carrying everything upstairs to the bath that he had fallen asleep before he could refill his basket.

"What-a-Mess!" He heard the angry voice of the woman of the house as she came downstairs. Perhaps she had found the jam he had accidently spilt on the stair carpet. He felt pretty sure she hadn't liked his idea with the bath. And the state of his room wasn't likely to go down too well either. It was time to beat a hasty retreat.

So there he was, sitting outside the house, wondering what to do next. He wanted very much to be kind and helpful, but it was obviously more difficult than he thought. "What-a-Mess!" the voice boomed again. What-a-Mess decided he had better try somewhere else to be helpful.

He wandered off down the street, and turned along a path that ran beside one of the gardens in the street. It had neatly trimmed privet hedges which had been cut into the shapes of various exotic birds. Suddenly he thought he heard a familiar voice. He stopped and listened. There it was again.

It seemed to be coming from the other side of the hedge, inside the garden. He listened carefully.

"Help," said the voice, weakly.

"Is that you, Cynthia?" asked What-a-Mess, recognising the voice of his hedgehog friend.

"Oh, Watty," whimpered Cynthia. "Am I glad to hear your kindly voice. Please help me. I'm trapped!"

At last! Someone who wanted him to be kind and helpful. Someone who was actually asking. The situation sounded desperate. There was no time to lose. What-a-Mess decided the most direct route was called for.

Without a thought for his own safety he began tearing his way through the hedge. Claws and teeth tore away like shoppers at the first day of the January sales, until at last he had succeeded in gouging out a space big enough for him to crawl through.

He saw Cynthia straight away. She was caught up in some netting over by the runner beans.

"Hold on!" said What-a-Mess. "I'm coming." So too was rather a lot of hedge which he trailed behind him as he ploughed his way directly through rows of cabbages, onions, carrots and potatoes.

Once at the runner beans he got to work. He tore up the poles that held the netting, and after a great deal of digging, biting, pawing and clawing, Cynthia was free.

"Oh, Watty," she said. "You're a hero, I've been here since last night. My hot water bottle's gone stone cold, and I've missed my breakfast. I thought I'd never free myself. I was about to give up. Thank you, thank you, thank you!"

This was more like it. This was what was supposed to happen when you were kind and helpful to people. What-a-Mess glowed with satisfaction at a deed well done. He felt so good that he even felt brave enough to go home.

He put up with being told off by the woman of the house. Cynthia's warm words of thanks gave him strength. The woman of the house finished telling him off and What-a-Mess spent the rest of

the day having several long zizzes all joined together to catch up on the sleep he'd missed the night before.

He woke up when the man of the house came home. It seemed that one of the neighbours had stopped him in the street. The neighbour was a very keen gardener. He grew all his own vegetables, but his pride and joy was his privet hedge. He had spent years training and trimming it into the shape of exotic birds. Now, apparently, it more closely resembled a modern sculpture on the subject 'Destruction of the Amazon Rainforests'. Without any exotic birds. Not one.

What-a-Mess heard 'hedge' mentioned. Then he heard 'cabbages' and 'onions' and 'carrots' and 'potatoes'. Then very loudly he heard the words 'runner beans'. Last, and loudest of all, he heard, "What-a-Mess!", and it didn't sound friendly at all.

Being kind and helpful was just about the most difficult thing he knew, decided What-a-Mess, as he crawled unhappily into the misery hole in the middle of the compost heap.

"What ho, Watty," said Cynthia, who was already snuggled up inside. "I brought you a bone as a thank you present." It was only a very small bone, but it was a kind thought.

At least somebody appreciated him, and What-a-Mess smiled as he gnawed happily at Cynthia's present.

Hide and Seek

What-a-Mess and his friends are playing hide and seek in the garden. Ryvita is having a hard job finding them. Can you help her find What-a-Mess, the Archbishop of Canterbury, the Cat-Next-Door, Cynthia and Poppet?

Make a Model

What-a-Mess and his friends have lots of fun playing together in the garden. Wouldn't it be great to be able to make up and act out their adventures for yourself? With the help of Mum or Dad, follow the instructions below to make your own scene and figures… here's how:

You will need:
several sheets of plain paper
cardboard
non-toxic glue
a ruler and pencil
round-ended scissors
coloured pens or paints

1. Stick the sheets of paper onto the cardboard.
2. With a ruler and pencil mark out a squared grid on each sheet. Make your squares 2.5cm by 2.5cm.
3. Copy the lines of the drawings onto your grids.
4. Colour the pictures in and cut them out.
5. Don't forget to leave the supporting tabs on to help the scene and figures to stand up. Glue these in place and assemble your models.
6. Take a large sheet of paper and draw and colour in your own garden path, lawn and vegetable patch. To make the model really sturdy glue this on to card, and then glue the model on to this garden base.

Make a Model

Finished model

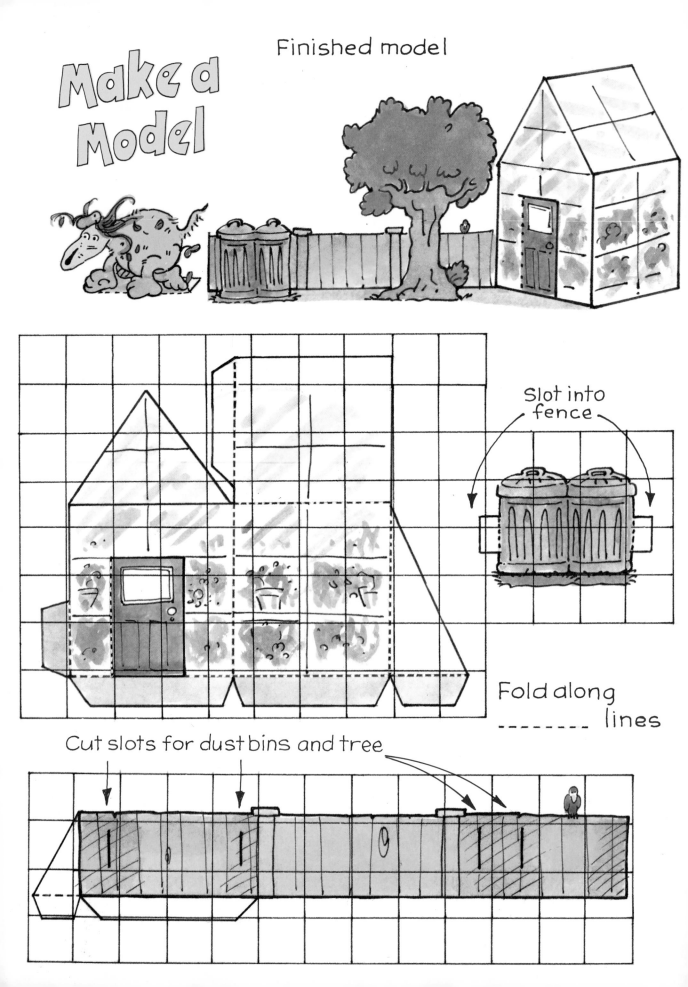

Slot into fence

Fold along
-------- lines

Cut slots for dust bins and tree

Back

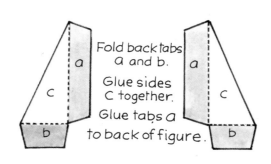

Fold back tabs a and b.

Glue sides C together.

Glue tabs a to back of figure.

Slot into fence

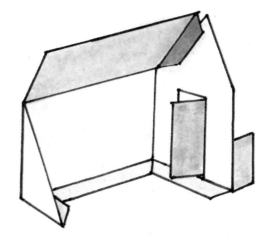

What-a-Laugh

The young boy stood watching a dog playing an accordion while a horse sang along to the music. "Fantastic," he said to the little girl next to him.

"It's nothing of the sort. That horse can't sing a note," scoffed the little girl. "The dog's a ventriloquist."

Patient: Doctor, I keep thinking I'm a dog.
Doctor: How long have you been feeling like this?
Patient: Ever since I was a puppy.

How many feet are there in a field of 340 sheep, 230 dogs, 105 horses, one sheepdog and a shepherd?

Two – the shepherd's. The dog has four paws, and all the rest have hooves.

What does the winner of a greyhound race lose?
His breath.

Man: Do you know the Battersea Dog's Home?
Friend: I didn't even know it had gone anywhere.

Why did the dog cross the road?
Because it was the chicken's day off.

Boy: It's raining cats and dogs outside.
Girl: I know it is, I've just stepped right into a poodle!

Husband: What kind of dog is that, dear?
Wife: It's a police dog.
Husband: But it doesn't look like a police dog.
Wife: Of course it doesn't! It's in the plain clothes division.

Basket of Delights

What-a-Mess's basket is full of all sorts of rubbish.
How many different things can you see beginning with S?
How many different things can you see coloured red?
How many different things can you see beginning with B?
How many different things can you see coloured green?

What-a-Mess and the Birthday Present

It was a black day. Some black days are a kind of dark grey, others are as black as liquorice. This day was so black that the thing it was as black as hadn't even been invented yet. A dark cloud hung over What-a-Mess's happiness. Little Poppet had come to stay.

If you were to draw up a list of the ten individuals What-a-Mess would least like to meet, Poppet would be nine of them. (The tenth was so horrible that What-a-Mess was very pleased he hadn't met it yet, and so didn't know who it was.)

The reason why What-a-Mess disliked Poppet was that she was a total disgrace to the name of dog. Anything that looked less like a dog, smelled less like a dog, and behaved less like a dog than Poppet would be hard to imagine. Of course, all the humans thought she was lovely, simply divine, and a joy to behold. It made What-a-Mess sick.

To begin with, Poppet was always beautifully groomed with not a hair out of place. If that wasn't bad enough she wore the most indescribably ugly bow on her head that made her look like a hairy helicopter. As to what she smelled of, it was like something that came out of a bottle and cost more than six weeks' pocket money, plus a month's wages for a paper round, and every last penny you had in your piggy bank.

It was an awful smell. No self-respecting dog would smell like that. The Archbishop of Canterbury thought it was probably a mixture of Channel Tunnel No. 5 and a bucket of sickly sweet, dead flowers. It was perfectly all right for a flower to smell like that, but a dog should smell like a dog, thought What-a-Mess.

The trouble was Poppet didn't really think of herself as a dog at all. She was "Mummy's little darling" or "a perfect little angel"; in short something rather special. She slept on a particularly plumply soft and sumptuous cushion. Occasionally she would deign to sample a little something from a tin, but she thought that rather vulgar, and by preference her diet consisted of freshly steamed fish, cooked meats and chocolates.

What-a-Mess was, of course, wildly jealous of the food, but what he objected to most was how she would turn up her nose at the most scrumptious dustbin delicacies. That, she firmly declared, was for creatures of an altogether lower order than she was. In other words, What-a-Mess and his friends.

All that was bad enough. So long as Poppet was a million miles away What-a-Mess didn't even think about her at all, except when he had bad dreams. But today the aunt of the man who lived in What-a-Mess's house had come to stay. And Poppet belonged to the aunt, so she had to come too.

This meant that What-a-Mess had to be washed and thoroughly groomed, which he hated. He was also supposed to be on his best behaviour. He couldn't watch television, play with the dustbins or allow Poppet to get even a teency-weency bit dirty.

What was even worse was that it was Poppet's birthday. She went on and on and on about it. In the end What-a-Mess had had enough. The trouble was he decided this in the middle of Poppet's special birthday tea. Just as he was about to tuck into a plate of roast beef Poppet declared that she hadn't invited him, and that it was all for her.

She snapped and barked and made such a dreadful racket that all the humans came running at once to see what the trouble was. Now not only was Poppet a greedy, pampered pet, she was also downright mean and cunning.

Just as the first human came into the room she rolled over, clutching her paw, and wailed as loud as ever she could.

Everyone immediately blamed What-a-Mess for biting, clawing or otherwise damaging precious little Poppet. To make matters worse, What-a-Mess watched in horror as all his roast beef was put on to her plate, and a generous helping of juicy gravy spooned over the lot.

What-a-Mess gave it up as a bad job and slunk off to be as miserable as he possibly could in his misery hole in the middle of the compost heap. But first, to cheer himself up a little, he rolled in the smelliest stuff he could find and generally scragged his coat about until it looked suitably scruffy.

The Cat-Next-Door was sympathetic. She remembered how Poppet had chased her and trapped her for over an hour in a mole hole. "What a beast," she said.

The Archbishop of Canterbury also came along to console his pal. Poppet had helped to glue his teeth together with a toffee on her last visit, so he knew the perils that What-a-Mess had to face. "What a horror," he said.

Together the three of them sat and were thoroughly glum. They thought up all sorts of schemes to help What-a-Mess get his own back, but it was no use. "They'll just blame me," What-a-Mess said, gloomily. "They always do."

Then the Cat-Next-Door had an inspiration. "What you need," she said, "is an alibi."

"But I don't want to go to sleep," said What-a-Mess, surprised that the cat should come up with such a useless and stupid idea in his hour of need.

"That's a lullaby," laughed the Archbishop of Canterbury.

"What's an alibi then?" said What-a-Mess.

"It's when you're somewhere else when the crime is committed," explained the Cat-Next-Door, "and someone is there to see you."

"Oh, I'd like one of those," said What-a-Mess. "Where can I get one?"

The Cat-Next-Door told him what he had to do. What-a-Mess nodded eagerly.

"All right," he said. "Leave it to me. You go and get Poppet's present ready."

While the Archbishop of Canterbury and the Cat-Next-Door made their preparations What-a-Mess went back to the house. Poppet was lounging on her cushion, recovering from her feast. What-a-Mess cast aside all thoughts of his roast beef inside Poppet's stomach, and put on his most polite and creeping manner.

"I do hope you enjoyed your birthday tea," he said. "You're such a very special dog you deserve everything you get. Just to show there's no hard feelings I want to give you a surprise present myself."

Poppet was so conceited she didn't realize that What-a-Mess was laying a trap for her. "What is

it?" she asked, lazily scooping up a chocolate from the box beside her, and not even offering one to What-a-Mess.

"Well it wouldn't be a surprise if I told you, would it?" said What-a-Mess, trying not to drool over the chocolates. "I've hidden it in a special place down the end of the garden."

"I'm so full," said Poppet, "I couldn't possibly walk that far."

"After all, it is *my* present."

What-a-Mess gave her directions and then raced off to find his mother. "Mother, I want to go walkies."

His mother looked at him in amazement. "You want to go walkies . . . on the *lead?*" she asked.

"Oh, yes please," said What-a-Mess. "I want to make up for all the trouble I caused. I'll be very good, very obedient."

With his mother's help he persuaded the man of the house to take him out for a walk on the lead. He walked to heel, instead of pulling the man down the street. He sat at the kerbside while they waited to cross the road instead of rushing out and causing accidents. And he didn't chase after anything, not even a tempting ice-cream wrapper that wafted by. All the time he was smiling inside, knowing that he had the perfect alibi.

At last they arrived back at the house. Inside they could hear the most terrible uproar. The woman of the house was jumping up and down, shouting, "I've been bitten. One of them bit me!"

The man's aunt was joining in. "There's another, and another!" she screamed. "There are hundreds of them. Ow! Ow! I've been bitten too." What-a-Mess sat obediently on the doorstep while the man went to investigate. A minute later he came out, shouting and scratching himself all over.

What-a-Mess knew how greedy Poppet was, however. "That's a pity," he said. "I suppose I'll have to have them all myself. It would be a shame to waste them." He made as if to go, licking his lips at the thought of some delicious treat that awaited him.

Poppet perked up at once. "I imagine I could manage a stroll to the bottom of the garden," she said in her sickly sweet voice.

"That awful Poppet has brought fleas into the house," he said to What-a-Mess after he'd stopped jumping up and down. "They're everywhere! Ow! Ow!" he added, and began to jump up and down again. "That dreadful, dreadful dog!" What-a-Mess sat there and grinned to himself.

That evening What-a-Mess was contentedly sharing a few juicy titbits with his friends, the Archbishop of Canterbury, the Cat-Next-Door, and Cynthia the hedgehog, whilst explaining what had happened. They could hardly eat for laughing (but they managed, of course).

"And so they had to have the whole house sprayed by the man from the council," said What-a-Mess, chewing on a particularly gravy-covered slice of meat. "Poppet had to be sprayed as well, and they threw away her bow and her cushion. Then they packed her off home."

"Good," said the Archbishop of Canterbury, licking his lips. "That bit of hedge at the bottom of the garden is usually good for a few fleas. And the Cat-Next-Door and I collected as many others as we could from all the cats and dogs in the neighbourhood. There must have been millions!" he laughed.

"And of course it couldn't possibly have been anything to do with you," said the Cat-Next-Door, "because you were out for a walk with the man of the house."

"So Poppet got all the blame," said What-a-Mess. "Perfect."

Just then Ryvita landed nearby.

"I couldn't agree more," said Cynthia, who was the only one who could hear Ryvita's tiny voice. "Every cloud does indeed have a silver lining."

Answers to Spot the Difference (page 32)

Ten things are missing in the second picture:
1. rabbit's tail; 2. yellow flower; 3. stone in the foreground;
4. tin can; 5. leafy twig; 6. handle on the bucket; 7. duck in What-a-Mess's hair; 8. spot on the Archbishop of Canterbury;
9. branch from rubbish heap; 10. hill in the background.

What-a-Mess

The Great

A game for 2-4 players. You will need four counters and a dice.

What-a-Mess and his friends have decided to have a race around the garden. Decide if you are going to play What-a-Mess, the Archbishop of Canterbury, the Cat-Next-Door or Poppet. Shake six to start and obey the instructions on each square you land on. If you throw six during the game you get an extra throw. If you land on an occupied square the player who was there first goes back to the start. First one past the finishing post wins.

Follow trail of Bones. Move on 5.

Smell lampost: Excitement moves you on 1.

START FINISH

Chase Postman move on 4.

Boy chases you Go back. 3

Chase a sweet wrapping Move on 2.

Find a bone: Take short cut.

Can't decide which way to go. Miss one turn.

Chased by angry neighbour. Go back 4.

Get stuck up tree: Miss one turn.

Frank Muir's What-a-Mess